Rhyme
Time

Red Riding
Hood Rap

First published in 2008 by
Franklin Watts
338 Euston Road
London
NW1 3BH

Franklin Watts Australia
Level 17/207 Kent Street
Sydney
NSW 2000

A CIP catalogue record for this book is available
from the British Library.

ISBN 978 0 7496 7947 7 (hbk)
ISBN 978 0 7496 7959 0 (pbk)

Series Editor: Jackie Hamley
Editor: Melanie Palmer
Series Advisor: Dr Barrie Wade
Series Designer: Peter Scoulding

Printed in China

Franklin Watts is a division of
Hachette Children's Books,
an Hachette Livre UK company.
www.hachettelivre.co.uk

Red Riding Hood Rap

by Penny Dolan

Illustrated by Desideria Guicciardini

W

FRANKLIN WATTS
LONDON • SYDNEY

See the little girl
in a red, red hood,

skipping through the trees
in the dark, dark wood.

Wicked old wolfie cries,
"Woo hoo hoo!"

"I've got the tummy rumbles
and I'm going to catch YOU!'

See the smiley granny
open up her door.

In jumps wicked wolfie
with a scary-wary roar.

But crafty old granny
starts to shout, shout,
shout!

"I'm safe in the cupboard and I won't come out."

Here's the wicked wolfie

hiding in the bed –

a silly, frilly night-cap
on his big wolf head.

But the clever little girly goes, "Hee hee hee!

You're a big bad wolfie
but you won't catch ME!"

Here's the girly

and the granny

and the woodcutter man,

all yelling at the wolfie
as loudly as they can!

Wicked old wolfie cries,
"Crick crick crack!"

"I'm going far away and I won't come back!"

Leapfrog Rhyme Time has been specially designed to fit the requirements of the Literacy Framework. It offers real books for beginner readers by top authors and illustrators.

Other Leapfrog titles also available:

Leapfrog Fairy Tales

A selection of favourite fairy tales, simply retold.

Leapfrog

Fun, original stories by top authors and illustrators.

For more details go to:

www.franklinwatts.co.uk